The Dressed-Up Rabbit

by
Gerda Muller

 GOLDEN PRESS · NEW YORK

WESTERN PUBLISHING COMPANY, INC.
RACINE, WISCONSIN

Kathy lived in the city, but her grandmother lived in an old house in the country. It was a pleasant place with an attic full of wonderful things for a little girl to play with.

Kathy loved to visit her grandmother, for in the country there were trees and flowers everywhere and lots of space to run and play. Best of all, Grandmother never told Kathy to be quiet when she wanted to laugh or shout or sing.

One day Grandmother came in her car to pick up Kathy and drive her to the country. On the way, Kathy asked, "How do you like my new doll, Grandmother? Do you think she'll fit into that old carriage in the attic?"

"I think so," said Grandmother. "But you'll soon find out, for I've brought the carriage down to the yard where you can play with it."

"Oh, Grandmother," said Kathy, "I love you very much. But before I play with the carriage, I'm going to go exploring."

Kathy was curious about the things she saw, and sometimes she dug up ants' homes with a stick. No one had told her it would be more fun to watch the little creatures at work.

Kathy liked the country, but somehow things always went wrong for her there. Though she tried to be careful, she snapped off twigs and trampled flowers. When she sang, it was at the top of her voice, for how was she to know this frightened the animals away?

Nor did she know how thin and delicate a butterfly's wings could be. And when she picked a bouquet of wildflowers for Grandmother, she pulled them up, roots and all. She had never heard that roots must be left in the ground if plants were to grow from them again.

After Kathy had explored for a while, she decided to go back to her Grandmother's cottage. "I'll take my new doll for a walk," she thought. But on the way she saw a little rabbit that was caught in a bramble bush. The tiny creature couldn't move. Kathy knelt down and carefully pulled away the branches of the bush, one by one.

When the bunny was free at last, Kathy lifted it in her hands. The frightened little animal struggled and tried to get away, but Kathy held onto it firmly.

"Grandmother! Grandmother!" she shouted as she ran toward the house. "See what I've found!"

But no one answered, for Kathy's grandmother had gone to the village to do her shopping. The little girl held the bunny close to her and wondered what to do next. At last she had an idea, and she whispered it to the bunny.

"I know what to do," she said. "We'll take a walk. I'll put you in my doll carriage, and we'll go to the village to meet Grandmother."

The bunny shivered. "I think you're cold," said Kathy, "and so I'll dress you up. Till then you can stay in this warm blanket."

Kathy first put the bunny in one of her doll's dresses, but he soon tried to wriggle out of it.

Next she tied booties to his paws, but try as he might, the poor bunny couldn't free himself.

Then Kathy wrapped him in a scarf. Poor bunny! He was almost suffocated by all those clothes on top of his own fur coat, and he grew more frightened.

14

After Kathy had tucked the bunny into the old carriage, she wheeled him off toward the village. As she walked along, she sang a song:

"Look, bunny! Do you see the flowers?

"Look, bunny! Look!"

But the rabbit couldn't see a thing. All he wanted to do was to get out of that carriage and scamper off into the fields.

Then, in the midst of her song, Kathy heard a voice calling: "Red! Here, Red!"

It was Mark, the boy who lived in a house nearby. He was out walking his dog, and when he saw Kathy he called a cheerful "Hi!"

"Hello, Mark!" she answered. "I'll bet you can't guess what I've got in my carriage."

"Let me think," said the boy. "Is it your teddy bear?"

Kathy shook her head.

"Well, then, it must be a frog," said Mark.

Kathy wrinkled her nose in disgust.

"Oh, I know," said Mark. "It's an elephant."

Kathy burst out laughing.

"You'll never guess," she said. "Come, have a look."

But Mark's big dog wanted
to see what was in the carriage, too.

"Stop pulling, Red !" Mark ordered.

Suddenly Red started to bark furiously, and he sprang at the carriage.

Over it went, and out tumbled the blanket, the pillows, and the little dressed-up rabbit. Off went the bunny, with Red close behind, dragging Mark after him.

It didn't take the little rabbit long to disappear into the woods, clothes and all, and when Kathy saw him go, she began to cry.

Red wagged his tail, begging forgiveness, and Mark did his best to console Kathy.

"Don't cry," he said. "I can fix your carriage. But you must remember that a rabbit is not a doll."

Just then Grandmother came up the path and asked what was wrong. When Mark had explained everything, Grandmother said, "Stop crying, Kathy, and see if you can't find your doll's clothes. The little rabbit must have lost them getting away."

Kathy was the first to find something – a bootie caught on a bramble bush.

Then Mark called, "Here's the scarf!"

At last the second bootie turned up. It was dangling from a twig that grew near a clump of ferns.

21

A little later they found the dress hanging on a bush. Then, suddenly, Mark stopped and pointed toward the roots of an old pine tree. "I'll bet your rabbit lives down there," he said. "He must have squirmed out of the dress just before he scooted into his burrow."

Kathy leaned over the rabbit's hole and called, "Come here, little bunny! Don't be afraid."

"Shhh!" Mark whispered. "Be quiet! You've scared him enough for one day. He's much better off with his mother."

Then Mark took Kathy by the hand and asked, "How would you like to see the other animals that live in the forest?"

"May we pet them?" asked Kathy.

"Of course not," Mark replied. "They're wild. We'll have to hide and not make a sound or they'll be frightened and run away."

And from their hiding place behind a bush here is what they saw. . . .

In the days that followed, Kathy learned from Mark the secrets of the woods and fields, and how the plants and animals live. She no longer pulled up plants and flowers by their roots, and she quietly watched the ants as they worked.

On the day Kathy was to leave, Mark had a surprise for her.

"Here is a little furry animal that loves to live in city houses," he said. "It's called a hamster. And here's a little book that will tell you how to care for it."

Kathy's grandmother also had a going-away present for her—a big book that told in words and pictures about animals from all over the world.

Back in her own home in the city, Kathy settled herself in a chair and opened her big book to the chapter on rabbits.

Turn the page and you will see what she read.

EUROPEAN WILD RABBIT
AND BUNNY

COTTONTAIL RABBIT

WILD RABBITS

Wild rabbits live almost everywhere in the world. They are smaller than their cousins, the hares, with shorter ears and shorter hind legs. Because of their short hind legs, rabbits cannot run as fast as hares. Rabbits use their paws to dig tunnels under the ground, and in these burrows they make their homes.

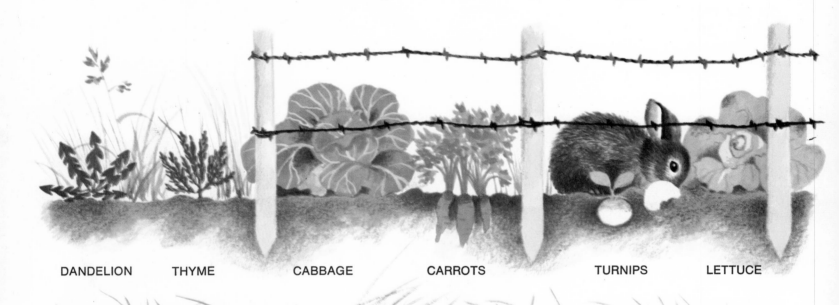

DANDELION   THYME   CABBAGE   CARROTS   TURNIPS   LETTUCE

THE NEST

Female rabbits, or does, dig separate underground rooms called *nests* for their babies, and it is here that the young bunnies spend several weeks while nursing. Later they learn by themselves how to find thyme and dandelion in the fields to eat. But what they like even better are vegetables from our gardens, and so, to protect their turnips, carrots, cabbages, and lettuce, farmers must drive away the rabbits.

28

BURROW

EAGLE

THE RABBIT'S ENEMIES

Many, many little rabbits are born each year, but not all of them have a chance to grow up. Natural enemies, like eagles and crows, threaten them from above, and on the ground martens, weasels, skunks, badgers, and foxes hunt them down, sometimes even going into their burrows. Human hunters with guns and dogs also track down rabbits to protect the crops and because rabbits make a very tasty meal.

MARTEN

FOX

DOMESTIC RABBITS

Domestic rabbits are related to wild rabbits and are raised on many farms where they are kept in *hutches*. There are more than 60 breeds of commercial rabbits, among them the *angora rabbit,* which is raised for its long, silky wool, and the *chinchilla rabbit* whose fur makes magnificent coats.

ANGORA RABBIT

HUTCH

RUSSIAN RABBIT

29